TWOCKING

by

Eric Brown

First published in Great Britain by Barrington Stoke Ltd
10 Belford Terrace, Edinburgh EH4 3DQ
Copyright © 2002 Eric Brown

The moral right of the author has been asserted in
accordance with the Copyright, Designs and
Patents Act 1988
ISBN 1-84299-042-X
Printed by Polestar AUP Aberdeen Ltd

A Note from the Author

I wanted to write a story about why teenagers steal cars, and what their actions can lead to.

Every year, in every city in Britain, thousands of cars are stolen. The joy-riders say, "We did it for the thrill. It's exciting. We were bored." But what happens when the excitement ends? What happens when the thrills run out?

This is the story of Joey and Emma and what happened when they came to the end of the road ...

To Susan Burke,
Niall and Declan.
And to Ann Dinsdale,
Emily and Joe.
Thanks.

Contents

Chapter 1
Emma's Fault?

It was Emma's fault.

If it wasn't for Emma, none of this would have happened. The deaths, the tragedy ... maybe even Emma would still be alive.

But it's easy to blame other people. I mean, though Emma was responsible, I could have done something to stop her. I should have said something, made her see how stupid it all was.

But I said nothing.

I often look back at what happened with me and Emma, and wonder why I didn't say something, why I just went along with what she suggested.

Why I went along for the ride ...

I'll tell you the whole story.

I didn't say anything then because I was having such a good time. I knew what we were doing was wrong, but it was also scary and thrilling – like nothing I'd ever done before.

I bet you're wondering what it was, aren't you?

Shoplifting? Stealing from houses? Mugging old ladies on their way home from Bingo?

No, none of those things.

It was more dangerous than any of them.

It was twocking.

Chapter 2
In the Park

We were bored, which was probably why
we did it. There was nothing else to do.
It was eight o'clock on a Monday night and
the telly was rubbish, and anyway, my dad
was in the house with his new woman. So I
couldn't go home.

We were in the park, about ten of us, just
mucking about. I didn't even have enough
money for a bottle of cider. Emma was
sharing her bottle of Diamond Ice with me,

and I was pretending to enjoy it, but I really only like Strongbow. So I just took small sips and acted drunk.

Skelly was really drunk, though. And when he was drunk he got nasty. Skelly was older than us, about 18. He was called Skelly because he looked like a skeleton, thin and white, with a little, hard head like a skull. There were rumours that he looked like that because he did drugs.

He staggered over to where I was sitting with Emma and punched my shoulder. Not hard, but almost hard enough to push me over the wall.

Emma caught me in time and said, "Why don't you get lost, Skelly. You're nothing but a pathetic moron!"

Skelly ignored her, staring at me. "Whassup, Joey Boy?"

I admired Emma for telling him to get lost. I wished I could do the same. I just looked away and tried to ignore him.

Skelly pushed me again. "What's she like, Joey? You two done it yet?"

The only light came from a street lamp about ten metres away. I was glad no-one could see my face, because it felt hot and red with embarrassment.

Skelly wouldn't give up. "Don't know why anyone would do it with fat Emma."

Before he could say anything else, Emma jumped up and punched him in the face, just like that. I heard the crack, and the next second, Skelly was lying on the floor, holding his nose.

Emma bent over him. "That'll teach you to call me fat in future!"

The others gathered around us, asking what had happened and looking at Skelly as if he was some kind of pond life.

We trailed through the park, leaving Skelly on the ground, moaning to himself. We sat on the bandstand and listened to the radio and mucked around.

Chapter 3
Emma and Me

Before Bradford Council closed the rec, we all used to meet there and play football. Emma was as good as any boy on the estate. She could tackle like David Batty and she had a shot like a cannonball.

Then the council sold off the land for a new housing estate. They opened a youth club up the street, but that only lasted six months.

It was OK – table tennis, table football, even pool. But some older kids got in one night and trashed the place. It was repaired, but they only did it again, so the council finally said, 'Why bother?' and closed the place down.

So then we met in the park, by the gents' toilets, or under the bandstand if it was raining.

Emma sat on the wall of the bandstand and swung her legs. She was watching me in the moonlight.

"What?" I said.

She pushed out her lips, popped her bubblegum. I could tell she was considering something.

For an awful second I thought she was thinking about what Skelly had said, about me and her, doing it.

Strange thing was, when I was on my own, the thought of having sex with Emma was kind of – I don't know – exciting, I suppose. But when I was with her I couldn't even think of it. I was too shy and embarrassed to know how to start. I mean, what did you say? How did you even begin to suggest something as amazing and frightening as having sex with someone?

She leaned over and pulled something from her pocket. She jingled it in front of me.

"What's that?" I asked, like an idiot. I could see that it was a bunch of keys.

"What do you think, Joey? It's a bunch of bananas."

"Keys," I mumbled. I thought, *her mum and dad are out, and she wants us to go back to her place and ...*

"Right," she said. "Keys. You want to go for a ride?"

"A ride?"

Emma laughed. "You sound like a parrot, Joey."

I just shrugged and said, "Sorry."

Emma kicked her legs and popped her bubblegum. She said, "You want to go twocking, Joey?"

I nearly said, "Twocking?" but stopped myself just in time.

I thought, *that's a strange name for having sex.*

"Come on, let's go!" She jumped from the bandstand and ran into the darkness. After a second, I followed her.

"Where you off to?" the others asked.

And from up ahead Emma shouted, "Twocking!"

Chapter 4

How We Met

I'll tell you how we first met, two years ago. We weren't always friends, Emma and me. To begin with, we were enemies.

Emma was the hardest girl I knew. She could beat up every boy in our year at school. People kept away from her. She wasn't a bully, but if anyone ever said anything to her about her weight – well, she'd go ballistic. God help anyone who got on her wrong side.

I met Emma when I was 13. She moved onto our estate, right next door to where I lived with my dad.

For the first week, we just looked at each other without saying a word. I didn't like the look of her. She was taller than me, and plump. She was quite pretty, I suppose – not that I could see that, then. I just saw an angry teenage girl who was unhappy about herself, and the only way she had of defending herself was to attack.

No wonder she found it hard to make friends.

About two weeks after she moved in, I was coming home on the school bus. I sat at the back as I always did. Mine was the last stop, and by then there was only one other kid on the bus. Emma.

When it got to my stop, I walked down the bus to get off and made the mistake of glancing at her.

She followed me off the bus, and five seconds later I felt something hit my backside. I thought she'd kicked me, at first. But when I turned around, she was swinging her school bag for another go.

"What were you staring at, Ginger?" she said.

"Dunno," I said, "they don't label scum like you." I turned away. I was proud of myself – for about half a second.

Then I thought she'd hit me around the head with a brick, but it was only her fist.

We dropped our bags and faced each other like boxers. "Come on, Ginger," she said. "You think you can do me?"

I'd never hit a girl before, and I didn't want to start now. But I was angry. I raised my fists, and she launched herself at me.

It was strange, that fight. I began by holding back, not wanting to hit her. And then, when I found out she could fight, I really tried to hurt her. We were rolling around on the floor like mud wrestlers.

It lasted about two minutes before we stopped, worn out.

She pushed me away and gasped for breath. I was glad of the chance to rest.

"Hey," she said, "you're not a bad fighter for a skinny ginger nut." There was something like respect in her voice.

"Not bad yourself," I said, "for a girl."

Then I turned and walked away, expecting to feel her fist hit the back of my head at any second. By the time I reached home, I felt like I'd won a small victory.

Next time we met, she said, "Just got *Tomb Raider*. Want to come round my house and play it?"

And we had been best mates ever since.

Chapter 5
TWOCKING!

"Where we going, Emma?" I called out after her as she left the park on the evening she showed me the keys.

"I told you – twocking."

"OK," I said, "I give up. Tell me. What's twocking?"

She turned to me in the fading light and grinned. "You'll see."

We left the park and walked through our estate. It was about nine o'clock and quiet – the sort of quiet you get on Monday night that feels like the end of the world. We hurried along the street. You could look through all the lighted windows and see the families inside, watching crap telly.

I felt excited, even though I didn't really know what we were doing. I thought of my dad on the sofa with Helen, watching *Who Wants to be a Millionaire?* I was glad I was out here with Emma.

She ran across the road and stopped by a parked car, looking up and down the street to make sure no-one was watching her.

Then she pulled the keys from her pocket and, as quick as you like, opened the door and slipped into the driver's seat.

I could only stare, open-mouthed.

"Don't just stand there!" she hissed. "Get in!"

"But, but ..." I began, climbing into the passenger seat.

My thoughts were in a whirl. I didn't even know Emma could drive. I mean, she was only 15.

I watched in amazement as she started the car. The engine spluttered and sprang into life. She did things with the foot pedals and the engine revved.

She grinned across at me. "Where do you want to go to, Joey?"

"Emma? How'd you learn to drive?"

"My brother taught me."

The car lunged forward and then stopped with a jolt.

"Ooops," Emma laughed. "I'll try again."

This time the car moved smoothly forward. Emma glanced into the rear-view mirror and we pulled away from the curb and drove down the street.

My heart was hammering.

"Whose car is it?" I asked.

"My brother's. He's in Majorca for a week. I nicked his car keys from the drawer when me and Mum were round feeding the fish yesterday."

I stared at her. "If the police catch us ..." I said. Fear gripped me.

"The police have got better things to do than nick a couple of joy-riders. They're out catching real criminals."

Emma put her foot down and we sped out of Bradford. I watched the houses flash by. We were moving faster than my dad ever drove.

I groped around for my seat-belt and quickly fastened it.

"Let's go up on the moors," Emma said. "You should see the view from up there. We'll get some Diamond Ice, enjoy ourselves."

I looked across at her. "Stealing a car, drink driving ..."

She took no notice and pointed to the ashtray. "There's a couple of quid in there. Hop out at the off-licence and get some cider."

We passed through a small village on the way to the moors and Emma stopped at the first offy she saw.

I look much older than 15, and I had no problem buying a two litre bottle of Strongbow.

Emma complained when I got back. "Thought I said Diamond Ice, dummy."

"Only had this," I lied.

"It'll do, I suppose."

We set off again, and ten minutes later we pulled off the road into a lay-by and stared out at the city lights spread out below us. Emma turned the radio on and we passed the bottle of cider back and forth. My heart had stopped hammering.

"How many times you done this then?" I asked.

"He only went on holiday yesterday," she said. "This is the first."

I remembered something. "So this is twocking?"

She grinned. "That's what the police call it. T-W-O-C-K-I-N-G. Taking – Without – Owner's – Consent. Twocking."

"What does the K stand for?" I asked her.

She punched me in the ribs, but playfully. "No idea," she said.

We stayed there for an hour, talking. I was still a bit nervous in case the police found us, but I think the cider helped to calm me.

At ten, Emma started the engine. "Better be getting back."

My head was spinning with the drink. "Sure you can drive?"

She giggled. "Just watch me!"

She shot off down the lane, the car weaving this way and that. I gripped the seat, laughing through my fear. I expected to see the headlights of an oncoming car at any second.

Somehow we made it back into Bradford without crashing into anything. We were in luck – not a police car in sight.

She pulled up outside her brother's house and cut the engine. We sat in the ticking silence, staring at each other in the light of the street lamps.

"Fancy doing it again tomorrow, after school?" she asked.

Perhaps it was the alcohol in me that made me nod my head and say yes.

Perhaps, if I'd said no, things might have turned out differently.

Chapter 6

Louise

After I left Emma, I walked around the estate for 20 minutes before going home. When I closed my eyes, it felt as if the whole world was spinning crazily around me. Outside my house I stopped and tried to act sober.

Then I let myself in with my key and crept past the lounge. I had hoped Dad and Helen would be in there, slobbed out on the sofa like Siamese twins.

Just my luck – they weren't in the lounge.

They were sitting round the kitchen table, and my sister Louise and her husband, Greg, were with them.

"So," Greg said. "The night owl returns. Been anywhere interesting, Joey?"

I never knew what he was on about half the time. Greg worked in computers and earned pots of money.

Dad said, "Cup of tea, Joey?"

I managed to say, "No, thanks. I'm tired. I'm off to bed."

"Hey," Louise said. "Don't forget it's my birthday next week. I want a nice, big present from my baby brother."

Louise said things like that all the time, but I didn't mind. She was ten years older than me, but she seemed to understand me like no-one else. When Mum and Dad split up, she talked with me for hours, telling me that one day everything would be OK.

She got up and went over to the fridge for the milk. She was pregnant – the baby was due any day now. The bump was so big and stuck out so far that she waddled like a duck. It was so comical I had to smile.

She came over and gave me a peck on the cheek. "Night, Joey." She pulled away and stared at me. She could smell the cider on my breath.

She winked and whispered, "Drink lots of water, OK?"

I managed to say goodbye and leave the kitchen without falling over, and went upstairs to the bathroom. I drank as much water as I could, and then went to bed.

I lay awake for ages. Every time I closed my eyes, the room began spinning like a washing machine on the fast cycle.

So I kept my eyes open and stared into the darkness. I thought about Emma, and the thrill of riding in a stolen car, and the fear.

I couldn't wait until we went twocking again.

Chapter 7
The Manchester Run

Next day on the bus to school, Emma whispered, "Meet me at eight, outside the park. OK?"

The day seemed to drag. The lessons were even more boring than usual. In double Maths, I thought I was going to go mad.

Emma wasn't on the bus going home. I wasn't surprised. She often bunked off school, and spent the afternoons wandering around the shopping centre.

Helen was in the kitchen, making the dinner, when I got in. She was OK, really – she tried to be friendly. It was just that she wasn't my mum.

I ate dinner on a tray in the front room, watching *Neighbours*, while Dad and Helen ate in the kitchen.

At ten to eight I was out the door and running to the park.

Emma was late. I kicked my heels for 15 minutes, wondering where she was. It began to drizzle with rain.

Just when I was going to give up and go home, I heard a car horn. Headlights dazzled me. Someone shouted, "Wake up, Joey! Get in."

I ran to the car and jumped into the passenger seat. "Thought you were never going to turn up," I told her.

"Had to meet someone," she said.

She drove off, heading out of town. "How'd you like to go to Manchester?"

"Manchester?" I said, as if she had suggested a trip to the moon.

"Yeah, you know – it's a big city. Has the best football team in the world."

She knew I supported Leeds. I took no notice of her. "Why Manchester?"

We raced out of the town. I held onto my seat and kept a lookout for police cars. The fizzy mixture of fear and excitement was racing through my body like a drug.

"Fancy earning ten quid?"

I looked at her. "Doing what?"

"Just coming to Manchester with me."

I shrugged. "If that's all I have to do ..."

She laughed and turned on the radio full blast.

29

The rain was coming down really heavy now. The wipers batted back and forth, blurring the windscreen. We raced down the slipway onto the M62 motorway and Emma moved into the fast lane.

I watched the speedometer climb past 50, past 60 ...

We hit 70 miles per hour, and Emma went even faster.

Outside, the central lights whipped by in a blur. We were doing nearly 80 miles an hour.

"Emma, if the cops see us, we're done for."

I thought she was going to say something sarcastic about me being chicken. But she saw the sense of what I was saying. We slowed down to 60 and moved into the middle lane.

An hour later we were crawling through the dodgy streets on the east side of Manchester. What a tip! Row after row of small redbrick buildings, industrial estates, grim-looking pubs, boarded-up shop fronts. No wonder the people here supported Man United – they had nothing better to do.

I told Emma this, and she slapped me across the face.

She turned the car into a side street, switched on the overhead light and peered at an *A to Z* map of the city.

We set off again, Emma glancing at the map from time to time. We turned down a series of roads like something out of *Coronation Street*.

"You going to tell me where we're going?" I asked.

"Shut up and you'll find out. We're nearly there."

A minute later she braked suddenly. We were parked next to some waste ground full of old prams and washing machines. Across the road was a row of run-down houses.

"This it?" I said.

Emma turned to me. "I'll be gone about five minutes, OK. Just stay here and look after the car."

"Look after it?"

"Just make sure it isn't nicked."

I started to ask her what I should do if a gang of 20 skinheads decided they wanted to joy-ride. But she was already out of the car and running across the street.

I watched as she hammered on a door. It opened. She slipped quickly inside. Where on earth was she going?

I tuned the radio to *Five Live*. It was the Monday night game. Everton against Ipswich. Ipswich were losing 2–0. Surprise, surprise. The commentator was saying that nothing could save them from the drop, now.

I closed my eyes, sat back, and listened to the match.

Chapter 8

The Contact

Everton were 3–0 up when the car door opened and Emma jumped in. "Hey, sleepyhead. Catch."

She threw a plastic bag into my lap and started the engine.

We drove off. "What is it?"

"Dunno. I'm just the delivery girl."
She reached out and turned the radio onto a music station.

I opened the bag. Inside was a big, square, brown paper parcel, done up tightly with glossy, brown tape. I shook it, but it didn't rattle. It was pretty heavy. "Who's it for, Emma?"

She glanced at me, then looked back at the road. "Contacts," was all she said.

I sat in silence on the way back, thinking.

I was jumpy. I looked around for police cars, sure that we'd be picked up. What if a neighbour had seen the car missing, and called the cops? They might be out looking for the car right now.

"Emma," I said at last. "These are drugs, aren't they?"

She laughed at me and turned the music up even louder.

"Emma!" I said.

"Listen, I don't know what they are. Someone asked me to pick a parcel up. Why should I bother about what's inside?"

We were a mile from home when I saw the police car.

I noticed it in a side street when we passed. It was one of those jam sandwich cars – white, with a red stripe along the side. I looked back, and my heart jumped when the car pulled out behind us. "Hell," I said.

"What is it?"

I jerked my thumb over my shoulder. "Police. They're following us."

Suddenly, the parcel on my lap felt like a bomb.

"Nothing to worry about," Emma said. She even laughed. I felt sick.

"Just drive carefully, OK?" I said. "Don't do anything stupid."

I turned and looked through the rear window. The cop car was about ten metres behind us, keeping pace. They knew we were twocking, I could tell.

We came to some traffic lights and stopped. The police car drew alongside.

I turned my head. The driver was looking across at me, cool as you like. Then he leaned forward, peering past me to get a closer look at Emma.

I nearly wet myself. This is it, I thought. We've had it. We're going to be caught in a stolen car, with a load of drugs.

What would Dad say when the cops knocked on the door? What would Louise think of me, her baby brother?

The next time I looked, the cop was staring straight ahead, talking into his microphone. This is it, I thought. We've had it.

Then the lights changed. Red. Amber. Green. Emma drove on – and the police car turned left.

I collapsed in my seat, drained of energy.

Emma was laughing. "You big ponce, Joey!"

I looked across at her, and grinned.

Two minutes later we stopped outside the park gates, and before I knew it someone was climbing into the back seat.

"Whassup, Emma? Nice car you got yourself."

Skelly poked his small, bony face between the seats and grinned at us both. Emma grinned back.

"You do the biz, girl?"

Emma took the parcel from me and passed it back to Skelly. "Hey, nice one!" he said.

He sat back and pulled something from the pocket of his jeans. When I looked, he was peeling £10 notes from a fat roll of cash.

He counted out £40 and handed it over to Emma. "Nice doing business with you, Emma. See you around, Joey Boy."

He jumped out and ran off into the darkness.

Emma turned to me and held out a ten pound note. "Easy money, Joey."

I hesitated, then took the tenner.

"Thought you didn't like Skelly?" I said.

"Can't stand the creep," she said. "But if he's paying me 40 quid to drive over to Manchester ..."

Emma started the car and drove home. At last I said, "They're drugs, aren't they?"

She shrugged. "Dunno. Nothing to do with me." She glanced across at me. "Hey, lighten up, Joey."

She parked the car outside her brother's house. Just as I was about to climb out, she said, "Tomorrow at eight, OK? Outside the park. We'll go on the moors again, buy some cider and listen to music."

I looked away. "I don't know," I said, and hurried home.

That night I lay awake for a long time. I told myself that what we had done was wrong. Twocking, drugs ...

But the strange thing was, in spite of the fear and the knowledge that we were breaking the law, I had enjoyed the thrill of what we had done. The danger only added to the excitement.

I knew I'd meet Emma outside the park at eight tomorrow night.

How could I stop myself?

Chapter 9
Twocking for Real

We went out every night until the end of the week.

Emma always picked me up outside the park, and we drove off into the country. Sometimes we went up to the moors and sat listening to music and drinking cider. Other times we just drove around, going to places we'd never been to before.

Then the fun came to an end. Emma's brother got back from his holidays and we were without wheels.

On Monday at school, Emma came across to me in the playground. "Eight o'clock outside the park, OK?"

"What we doing?"

She grinned at me. "What do you think, Joey? We're twocking."

Before I could say anything, she ran off.

That night at eight, I hung around outside the park, my heart hammering like crazy. More than anything I wanted to go joy-riding again, even though a tiny voice in my head told me that it was wrong.

Emma was 30 minutes late.

A big car turned around the corner and sounded its horn. I stared. Emma was in the driving seat, waving at me to hurry up.

She swung open the passenger door and shouted. "Don't touch the door!"

"What? Why?" I eased myself into the seat without touching anything.

Emma passed me a pair of gloves. "Put these on, then close the door."

I did as she said. She started the car and we drove off, heading towards the moors. I felt my pulse quicken with the familiar, thrilling sense of danger. I looked around at the fancy interior of the car. It was a big Rover, with leather seats and a wooden dash. "Where'd you get this, Emma?"

"Twocked it from Rosebury Close," she said. "Easy as pie."

"They just left the key in the ignition?"

She snorted. "Nah. I know how to get into locked cars, Joey. I know how to start 'em, even."

43

I stared at her. "You do?"

"Skelly showed me. He knows all the tricks."

We parked on the moors overlooking the city. "It'll be more dangerous from now on, Joey. I mean, we're really twocking now. If the owners discover their car gone, the police'll be looking for it."

She stopped, and the silence was incredible. I could even hear my heart beating.

"You can drop out any time you like. I'll understand. I don't want to get you into trouble. But it'd be great if you could come along."

I grinned at her. "Try stopping me," I said.

She looked at me for a long time, then said, "Give us a kiss, Joey."

Chapter 10
All Good Things ...

The next few weeks were the happiest of my life. Most nights Emma would meet me with a different car and we'd speed around the countryside. We always ended up somewhere quiet and dark, and we'd kiss and play around while the radio belted out loud music.

Twice a week we went to Manchester and picked up a parcel for Skelly. When we did this, we'd catch a bus from Bradford to a town nearby and nick a car from there. Emma explained that it would be safer that way.

The police would soon be on our trail if the cars were all twocked from Bradford.

When we got off the bus we'd find a quiet street and stroll along until Emma came across a car she liked the look of. Then she'd pull a long, flexible wire from inside her jeans and slip it down between the car window and the door.

Seconds later we'd be inside, and I'd shine a torch beneath the steering wheel while Emma pulled off a plastic panel and played about with a mass of wires. Most times, the engine would splutter into life and we'd be off.

We'd dump the car somewhere on the way back from Manchester and take the bus to Bradford. We'd meet Skelly and get our money. Then we'd walk back home, drunk with cider, holding each other and singing.

As I said, it was the happiest time of my life.

But all good things come to an end ...

Chapter 11

Drugs

I started to notice that Emma was acting strange.

She was kind of dreamy and far away. She bunked off school a lot, and when I asked her what she did when she wasn't at school, she just shrugged her shoulders and said, "Nothing, just messing about."

Once she arranged to meet me at eight, to go twocking, but she didn't turn up. I felt sick, wondering what she was doing, who she was with. Had she found someone else?

Next day, she whispered to me during History, "Tonight at eight, OK? The park."

"You sure you'll turn up this time?"

"Sure I'm sure. Look, I'm sorry about last night. I just couldn't make it."

"Who were you with?"

She looked away. "No-one. Dad wouldn't let me out." But by the way she was acting, I knew it was a lie.

So at eight I turned up at the park, but there was no sign of Emma. *Not again*, I thought.

Then I heard the sound of an engine, and a car horn. "Joey!" Emma cried. "Hop in!"

The sight of her, waving from the window of a shiny new BMW, filled me with excitement.

"Where we going, Emma?" I asked as I climbed in.

She put her foot down and we raced out of Bradford. "Manchester. There's some cider in the back. You want some?" She seemed a bit drunk already.

So I opened the bottle and took a few gulps.

"Aren't you going to give me some?" she asked.

"While you're driving?"

"I haven't crashed yet, have I?"

I passed her the bottle and she took a big gulp or two. I know I shouldn't have let her have any more. But I was weak. I wanted to keep Emma as my girlfriend, you see.

She lowered the bottle, almost spilling it, and laughed. We swerved towards the side of the road, almost hitting a parked car, and my heart thumped with fright.

I held onto the seat for the rest of the journey, praying that we'd make it in one piece. I left the cider on the floor by my feet. I wanted another drink, but I didn't want Emma to get any drunker than she already was.

We reached Manchester safely and Emma picked up the parcel.

On the way back I asked her about where she went when she wasn't at school.

"I told you, Joey. We just mess about."

"We?"

"Just friends."

"Who?"

She looked across at me, her eyes on fire. "What's it got to do with you, Joey? You aren't my dad, are you?"

That hurt. I thought we had something, me and Emma. I suppose I was jealous, and I didn't like the feeling.

We met Skelly outside the park. He jumped in the back and rubbed his hands together.

Emma passed him the package and he pulled out a wad of notes from his back pocket.

He peeled off a tenner and passed it to me. "And this is for you, Emma." He passed her a small silver foil package about the size of a matchbox.

I just stared at her.

When Skelly got out, I said, "What is it, Emma?"

She glared at me. "What do you think?"

I managed to say, "He's paying you in drugs, isn't he?"

"What if he is? What's it got to do with you?"

"It's dangerous. You don't want to get into that."

"What do you know about it? I know what I'm doing. It isn't dangerous – it's fantastic. You don't know how wonderful it is until you've tried it ..." She looked at me.

I was tempted to give it a go, I can tell you. I mean, Emma didn't look ill, like you imagine drug addicts to be. She was just a bit dreamy, distant.

I shook my head. "I've got to get back."

She reached over and took my hand. "Let's go to the moors tomorrow, OK? Take a car and some drink and watch the city lights ..."

I smiled at her. "That'd be great."

She pulled me close. "Give us a kiss, Joey."

Chapter 12

Heart to Heart

On Friday night I was lying on my bed, listening to the latest Offspring album, when someone knocked on the door.

"Can I come in?" It was Louise. I turned the music down and opened the door.

Louise waddled in. She seemed even bigger today. Her tummy stuck out like a giant egg. Surely the baby would pop out soon. She sank into the chair by the bed with a sigh. "Ah, that's better."

I knew something was up. Normally, she never came into my room. The way she was looking at me – it was tender and concerned at the same time.

"Joey ..." she began.

"What?" I looked away, embarrassed.

Perhaps she'd seen me in a car with Emma? The thought filled me with fear. My face burned.

"Are you OK? I mean, is everything OK?" She was finding this as hard as I was.

"Everything's fine, Lou."

"Are you sure? You seem, I don't know, different these days. And – look, Dad's worried. He's noticed you've been buying things. Games, CDs."

She stopped, and stared at her hands which were folded on top of her huge bump. "Where are you getting the money from, Joey?"

I was quick with the lie.

"It's OK, Lou. They're all secondhand things," I said. "Bought them from kids at school. Dad didn't think I got them new, did he?" I laughed.

She smiled. "You're in a world of your own these days," she said. "Where do you go every night? Dad says you go out just before eight, every night."

"I'm seeing a friend," I said. "She's called Emma."

She looked surprised. "Oh," she said, and smiled. "Oh, I'm pleased." She seemed amazed that her little brother had a girlfriend.

I changed the subject. "When's the baby due?" I said, pointing.

"Yesterday," she laughed. "If nothing happens in the next couple of days, then I'm going into hospital and they'll bring it on. Are you looking forward to being an uncle?"

Before I could answer, Dad called up from the hall. "Phone, Joey."

55

I helped Louise up from the chair and ran downstairs. "Hello?"

"Joey? Emma here." She seemed dazed, dreamy. "You coming out tomorrow? We're going to Manchester."

Louise came down the stairs, smiling at me. I went red. She went into the lounge, and I could hear her and Dad, talking.

"Joey, you still there?"

"I'm here."

"Well, you up for it?"

"Sure," I said.

"Great. Meet you outside the park. Usual time, OK?"

How was I to know that this would be the very last time we'd go twocking?

How was I to know that, if I'd said 'no' to Emma, then everything would have been different?

Chapter 13

End of the Road

On Saturday night I hurried from the house and ran to the park. Emma was late, again. I was afraid that she wouldn't turn up. Then I saw headlights in the distance.

She pulled up beside me in a brand new Ford and waved at me through the window.

I knew the car from somewhere – but I thought nothing more about it, at the time.

I jumped into the passenger seat and Emma roared off.

I could tell that she was already drunk. Empty bottles of Diamond Ice rattled around at my feet. She was laughing as she took the corners at speed.

"Emma!"

"What?" she said. She sounded aggressive.

"It's Saturday night."

"So what?"

"So there'll be more cops out tonight, looking for drink-drivers."

She took no notice of me. We raced out of Bradford, towards the moors.

"Hey, Joey. Guess what I've got for you?"

I held onto the dash as we lurched around a corner. "What?"

"A little present from Skelly."

"Skelly can keep his little presents," I said.

"Come on, Joey. Why don't you try it? Just the two of us. We'll park above the city and share a wrap ..."

I hesitated. "What is it?"

"The big H," she said.

I stared at her. "Heroin?" I whispered.

"What did you think it was?" she asked. "So, do you want to try some?"

I shook my head. "No way. You're crazy."

"And you're chicken, Joey! You don't know how to enjoy life." She put her foot down on the accelerator and we sped down the narrow lane.

"Emma!"

"See! You're chicken!" She laughed aloud and went even faster.

We were careering all over the wet road, Emma laughing crazily as she pulled the steering wheel this way and that.

If a car came in the opposite direction now, we'd be shredded.

"Emma!" I began. And then I heard the siren.

I turned in my seat and stared through the rear window. A police car's flashing light turned the darkness bright blue. I yelled out in panic.

"Stop!"

Emma was mad. She just laughed even more and drove even faster.

"Emma, stop. If we stop now and run, we might get away!"

"I'm not running, Joey! I'm going to race them! Don't worry, I'll beat them!"

I looked back again. The police car was falling behind as Emma accelerated. Perhaps she was right, and we would get away.

We were racing along a straight lane, with a stone wall on our right, and on our left a drop of about ten metres. I'd never been as scared in all my life.

We turned a corner – and the lane became a pot-holed farm track. We hit a hole and swerved crazily. Emma stamped on the brakes and we came to a sudden stop.

"Get out and run!" I cried.

I pulled open the door and dived out. I staggered through the darkness. Behind us, I could see the headlights of the police car swerving around the bend.

I fell into a ditch and hid myself. I yelled at Emma again to get out and run, but she took no notice.

Instead, she started the engine and reversed. She turned the car, revved the engine, and accelerated back down the lane.

She was heading straight for the oncoming police car, and she wasn't slowing down.

I stared. I couldn't believe what I was seeing.

The two cars shot towards each other – and at the very last second, Emma swerved.

I watched as the car left the road and dropped away from sight.

Seconds later I heard the explosion and saw the orange ball of flame rise high into the air. I screamed. I was terrified.

I ran along the ditch towards the drop, then rolled through the bracken.

When I came to my senses, I was about 20 metres from the burning car. It was upside down, like a stranded beetle. Greedy flames swept over it.

But the worst thing of all were the screams.

As I stared in horror, I could hear Emma's screams as she burned to death.

I ran. I turned and sprinted through the bracken towards home. I fell over and picked myself up, and then fell over again.

I was yelling and crying and telling myself, over and over, that I should have done something.

Emma was dead, and I could have done something to prevent that ...

****

I bet you're thinking that this is the end, right?

Wrong.

Dead wrong.

When I thought that things couldn't possibly get worse, they did. They got a lot worse.

What could be worse than a death? I'll tell you ...

Two deaths.

Chapter 14
More Tragedy

It was late when I got home. I crept in the front door, left my trainers in the hall and made my way across to the stairs.

The light was on in the kitchen, and the door was open. I looked in, and I'll never forget what I saw.

Dad was sitting at the table, staring down at his hands. His face was white, and his eyes were red as if he'd been crying.

Helen was standing behind him, a hand on his shoulder. They looked up at the same time and saw me. I knew, then, that something terrible had happened. I found myself drifting towards them like in some awful dream.

They stared at me without saying a word.

"What is it?" I asked. "What's happened?"

At first, I thought that they must have found out about the car and the accident.

Then Dad said, "It's Louise."

I felt as though someone had punched me in the belly. I sat down suddenly. "What?" I said. "Is she OK?"

Dad started to speak, but the words wouldn't come.

Helen said, in a small voice, "Louise is OK now, Joey. But she lost the baby."

I felt tears stinging my eyes.

"How?" I said. "I mean, what happened?"

"The labour pains started, and the baby was on its way. But something went wrong – she was bleeding a lot ..." Helen said, then began crying and couldn't go on.

"The ambulance," Dad managed to say at last. "The ambulance took nearly an hour to arrive. All that time she was lying on the kitchen floor, bleeding. If the ambulance had arrived sooner, they could have saved the baby."

"But," I began, "why didn't Greg drive her to the hospital?"

I stopped, feeling suddenly sick. The car. The car that Emma had twocked. I thought I'd seen it before ...

Dad was shaking his head. "When Greg went to fetch the car," he said, "it was gone.

Someone had stolen the bloody car. So he rang for an ambulance, and it didn't turn up for almost an hour!"

He broke down, held his head in his hands, and wept.

Chapter 15
The Worst Day of My Life

It was Emma's fault.

If it wasn't for Emma, none of this would have happened. The deaths, the tragedy ... maybe even Emma would still be alive.

Maybe Louise would have a baby, now.

But it's easy to blame other people, and not yourself.

I know, in my heart, that I'm to blame too. I should have been strong enough to tell Emma that she was doing wrong.

Tomorrow I'm going to visit Louise in hospital. It should have been a great moment for both of us, but instead I know that it'll be the worst day of my life.

What will I say? How will I be able to act all warm and sympathetic, and at the same time hide my guilty secret?

Barrington Stoke would like to thank all its readers for commenting on the manuscript before publication and in particular:

Isabel Agnew
Eileen Armstrong
Joshua Ashman
Mrs J. Barrow
Jenna Braddon
Daine Brown
Shennáe Bryden
Louise Burton
Daniel Chapman
Emma Chapman
Kath Cox
Roger Cox
Joanna Douglas
Samantha Duff
Michael Freeman
Madonna Harnett
Emma Herron
Leanne Hollister
Kathryn Howes
Liz Hurley

James Johns
Psalm Lockwood
A. Martin
Donna Murray
Holly Northey
Samantha Owen
Alison Provis
Sarah Roberts
Sarah Rose
Julia Rowlandson
Miles Rudland
Ben Selby
Kath Simpson
Sharon Smith
Alex Smith
Annette Speak
Mathew Stacey
Vicki Standinger
Craig Taylor

Become a Consultant!

Would you like to give us feedback on our titles before they are published? Contact us at the e-mail address below – we'd love to hear from you!

E-mail: info@barringtonstoke.co.uk
Website: www.barringtonstoke.co.uk

More Teen Titles!

Joe's Story by Rachel Anderson 1-902260-70-8
Playing Against the Odds by Bernard Ashley 1-902260-69-4
Harpies by David Belbin 1-842990-31-4
To Be A Millionaire by Yvonne Coppard 1-902260-58-9
All We Know of Heaven by Peter Crowther 1-842990-32-2
Ring of Truth by Alan Durant 1-842990-33-0
Falling Awake by Vivian French 1-902260-54-6
The Wedding Present by Adèle Geras 1-902260-77-5
Shadow on the Stairs by Ann Halam 1-902260-57-0
Alien Deeps by Douglas Hill 1-902260-55-4
Dade County's Big Summer by Lesley Howarth 1-842990-43-8
Runaway Teacher by Pete Johnson 1-902260-59-7
No Stone Unturned by Brian Keaney 1-842990-34-9
Wings by James Lovegrove 1-842990-11-X
A Kind of Magic by Catherine MacPhail 1-842990-10-1
Clone Zone by Jonathan Meres 1-842990-09-8
The Dogs by Mark Morris 1-902260-76-7
Turnaround by Alison Prince 1-842990-44-6
Dream On by Bali Rai 1-842990-45-4
All Change by Rosie Rushton 1-902260-75-9
The Blessed and The Damned by Sara Sheridan 1-842990-08-X

Barrington Stoke, 10 Belford Terrace, Edinburgh EH4 3DQ
Tel: 0131 315 4933 Fax: 0131 315 4934
E-mail: info@barringtonstoke.demon.co.uk
Website: www.barringtonstoke.co.uk